# Fantastic Yak

Written and illustrated
by Laura Hambleton

**Collins**

Yak was sad.

Yak met Fox.

His sock had a rip.

6

Yak met Chicken.

Her pot had a chip.

chop

pat

12

13

/y/

14

  # After reading

**Letters and Sounds:** Phase 3

**Word count:** 40

**Focus phonemes:** /x/ /y/ /ch/ /th/ /nk/

**Common exception words:** I, was, you, her

**Curriculum links:** Understanding the World: The World

**Early learning goals:** Listening and attention: listen to stories, accurately anticipating key events and respond to what is heard with relevant comments, questions or actions; Understanding: answer 'how' and 'why' questions about experiences and in response to stories or events; Reading: children use phonic knowledge to decode regular words and read them aloud accurately; they demonstrate understanding when talking with others about what they have read

## Developing fluency

- Your child may enjoy hearing you read the story.
- Model reading with lots of expression. Take turns to read a page. Ask your child to say the 'sound effect' words on pages 7 and 11 and accompany each word with an action.

## Phonic practice

- Point to the word **chip** on page 9 and practise the sound /ch/. Model sounding out the word ch-i-p and ask your child to copy you. Do the same with the word **thank** on page 13.
- Now look at the I spy sounds on pages 14 and 15 together. Which words can your child find in the picture with the x and y sounds in them? (e.g. *fox, boxes, six, yak, yolk, yacht, yellow*).
- Practise together sounding out words with more than one syllable. Read the sounds in each syllable 'chunk' and blend.

chick/en

fan/tas/tic

## Extending vocabulary

- Ask your child:
  - Do you know what the word **fantastic** means?
  - Can you think of another word that means the same thing as **fantastic**? (*great, wonderful, excellent*)
  - What word would you use to describe Yak?